THE COMBINATION

ELIAS CARR

NIGHT FALL

THE COMBINATION

ELIAS CARR

MINNEAPOLIS

Darby Creek
A division of Lerner Publishing Group, Inc.
241 First Avenue North
Minneapolis, MN 55401 U.S.A.

Website address: www.lernerbooks.com

Cover photograph © iStockphoto.com/Adam Korzekwa.

Main body text set in Momento Regular 12/16.

Library of Congress Cataloging-in-Publication Data
Carr, Elias.
The combination / by Elias Carr.
    p.   cm. — (Night fall)
Summary: On the hundredth anniversary of the erection of a
high school building by an architect considered to be insane, the
misdialing of locker combinations may turn the structure into a
gateway to hell unless students Dante, Miranda, and Vincent can
help historian Dr. Spangler stop it.
ISBN 978-0-7613-7742-9 (lib. bdg. : alk. paper)
[1. Supernatural—Fiction. 2. High schools—Fiction. 3. Schools—
Fiction. 4. Horror stories.] I. Title.
PZ7.C229323Com 2011
[Fic]—dc22   2011000961

Manufactured in the United States of America
1—BP—7/15/11

Deep into that darkness peering, long I stood there wondering, fearing,
Doubting, dreaming dreams no mortal ever dared to dream before

—Edgar Allan Poe, The Raven

Miranda Lee woke up sweating. That dream again. The one where everyone laughed and pointed as she tried and tried to get her locker open. In the dream she couldn't even focus her eyes on the combination written on her schedule. She pulled the covers over her head.

"Rise and shine!" her mom sang out, coming into her room and snapping up the shades. "Big first day of someone's junior year! The journey to the right college begins today!"

When Miranda shuffled out of her room wearing her school uniform, her dad stuck his head out of the bathroom. His face was half covered in shaving cream.

"Our little girl is starting a big year!" he crowed. "Want to know my locker combination from first semester my junior year?"

"Not really," Miranda muttered.

"Scorpion, fish, twins, bull, lion, crab, lion. I took it as lucky sign for my love life that year," he chuckled. "Maybe Mrs. Konstantinos will give you a good one, too. Tell Ma I'm almost ready for breakfast."

Miranda sighed and plodded down the hall.

While his mom stared at the TV, Dante Grant cracked a second egg into his protein smoothie. He was the first sophomore in years to make the St. Philomena High varsity football team. He knew he'd made the team because he was fast. He also knew if he wanted any real playing time, he'd have to be fast—and a lot bigger.

As he gagged down the smoothie, the TV

caught his eye. It was the local morning show. As usual, it had annoying, way-too-awake hosts chatting in a stupid fake living room. At the moment, though, the camera was slowly panning over the outside of St. Philomena High. The camera paused on the weird gargoyles and carvings on the roof.

"The high school is one of Bridgewater's most significant buildings," said a perky reporter, "and this first day of school marks the one hundredth anniversary of the building's opening." The camera zoomed in on a row of tall, arched windows on the second floor. They were protected by iron bars. "Famed architect Ivor Shandor only built two buildings in the United States, one at 55 Central Park West in Manhattan and the other here in Bridgewater. Most of the building materials and fixtures came from local sources. But the unusual locks and lockers Shandor insisted on importing from a factory in his home country of. . . ."

Dante chugged down the last of his shake. If he was going to hit the weight room, he had to get moving. First day of classes didn't matter. He had real work to do.

"Bye, Mom," he said as he headed to the door, his backpack over one shoulder.

"Bye," his mother replied a moment later. She was still looking at the TV. The reporter was now interviewing a man in glasses and a tweed jacket. He had a British accent and seemed nervous.

"Shandor was a genius, of course, but he was also a bit of a madman. For instance, he had very unusual ideas about the end of the world. . . ."

Black-and-white tile covered the floor of the basement of St. Philomena High, where echoing hallways opened into locker rooms, storage closets, and the weight room. In the center of the basement was the pentagon-shaped boiler room. On each wall was an arched steel door. Instead of a handle, each door had a huge wheel.

Dante had no idea how those wheels-for-door-handles were supposed to work. He'd been in the boiler room, but he'd never had to open the doors.

To call the enormous boiler room "creepy" was like calling *Saw III* "kinda scary." Leaving a freshman wrapped in athletic tape in the middle of the dark boiler room was a long-standing St. Philomena football tradition. Dante remembered it very clearly from last year.

He was a little proud of how he'd done as the "freshman mummy." The seniors had picked him up—wearing only a towel—blindfolded him, wrapped him in tape, and dumped him in the dark boiler room. The last one to leave had yelled "Come on, Flash. Let's see you run out of this." And then he was gone. When the echo faded, only the low hum and rattle of the machines had remained in Dante's ears.

It only took him a minute or so to wiggle out of the tape and rip off the blindfold. He was still wet from the shower, so that was easy enough. The trick had been finding his way out in the total darkness. The room was full of ancient-looking heating equipment, tools, and random bits of iron he didn't want to run into nearly naked. Despite what the senior had said, it hadn't been the time to use his speed.

Reluctantly, Dante had removed his towel and snapped it out in front of himself like a whip, figuring it would keep him from walking into something. He had taken three steps before he felt his towel hit something and catch. He pulled the towel back and felt it tear.

"Son of a—!" His voice echoed back at him. He had carefully turned around, holding half a towel, and tried the other direction.

This time he was luckier. His towel hit something—a wall. After spending forever groping along the wall, he found the right spot. Cautiously, he removed the vent and clambered through. As he blinked in the bright light, he felt relieved to see he was in the locker room.

Then he'd seen a couple of girls in volleyball uniforms come around the corner and realized which locker room he was in. He was in the girls' locker room, naked, with only half a towel.

That had been the moment to run.

On the first morning of the new school year, Dante didn't have to worry about being hazed.

Not only had he made varsity, he was also the only one in the locker room.

"Everyone else is so lazy," he said to himself, turning the dial on his lock. "I'm starting every game this season," he continued, yanking the latch for emphasis. The combination must have been wrong, because it refused to budge. "Man, I hate these things. Why can't we have normal locks?" Dante said, a little quieter this time. He spun the dial once again.

Somewhere deep in the boiler room, though, something did click. Dante didn't hear it, but someone else did.

Miranda tried to slow down as she approached the front doors of the school. Back when she was a freshman, she'd run to every class because she didn't want to be late. Her classmates lounging in the halls would snicker as she anxiously speed-walked past.

"Nerd," they'd say . . . or worse. But when they slouched in right before the bell rang, Miranda already had her desk perfectly arranged: notebook open, and a freshly sharpened pencil in her hand. Another sharp pencil parallel to the top of the page, and her lucky eraser in the upper left-hand corner of the desk. Trouble was, no one seemed much impressed.

Now, as a junior, Miranda had learned to try to be a little cooler. But it was still hard work. She didn't get teased as often, though people still muttered about how she threw the curve in every class. She even had a boyfriend.

Miranda frowned, thinking about Vincent. She had been so excited last year when she found out he liked her. The last month of school had been a blur of passing notes in social studies and texting every night. But then she got a 96 on her social studies final. Any cool quota she'd built up that year had been blown when she burst into tears in front of the whole class. And her mom had had a talk with her about "distractions" and her older sister's full scholarship to Harvard. . . .

This year she had to apply herself to school like never before. This was the year that really counted with colleges, and she wasn't going to let anything stand in the way of getting into an Ivy League school.

Even though there were still twenty minutes before homeroom, Miranda couldn't help hurrying as she walked toward the library. Only a few other kids were there, picking up their schedules from Mrs. Konstantinos, the school librarian.

Usually Miranda loved libraries and was a favorite with librarians. But Mrs. Konstantinos never seemed to remember Miranda, or anyone else for that matter. There had been a Mrs. Konstantinos at St. Philomena back when Miranda's father was in high school. He said she'd died. That this Mrs. Konstantinos was the other one's daughter or something. It didn't make any sense to Miranda. Once she'd looked in the St. Philomena yearbook from the year her dad had graduated. The picture of Mrs. Konstantinos looked exactly the same. She'd looked in yearbooks even further back and found the same thing. And once, she'd just been paging through the yearbook from the year St. Philomena opened when Mrs. Konstantinos had spoken behind her.

"What are you doing?"

Miranda had jumped a mile, slammed the

book shut, and murmured something about a report on St. Philomena history. But she was sure she'd seen a picture of Mrs. Konstantinos in the staff section that exactly the same as all the others for the last hundred years.

As Mrs. Konstantinos looked for Miranda's schedule, Miranda stared at the big, black, leather-covered book chained to the desk. Supposedly no one other than Mrs. Konstantinos had ever looked inside. It contained Miranda's only real nemesis at St. Philomena High—the locker combinations. Math problems, English papers, badminton serves—all these Miranda knew she could conquer with hard work and her high IQ. But she'd never mastered the stupid locker combinations here. Worst of all, everyone switched lockers every semester. She was constantly trying to learn new combinations.

Everyone knew—Miranda better than most, because she really had written a report on St. Philomena High's history—that the lockers at the high school were one of its unique features. Instead of numbers, the locks embedded in the locker doors had strange astrological hieroglyphics on them. Each combination was a seven-symbol sequence.

Mrs. Konstantinos's book held the combination for each locker in the school. When the school office printed off the student schedules, it left the box for the locker combination empty. The stack of schedules was then delivered to Mrs. Konstantinos by the student office aide. Mrs. Konstantinos assigned a locker and wrote down the combination on each schedule. Miranda had always been assigned lockers down by the gym, far from most of her classes.

With a thin smile, Mrs. Konstantinos handed Miranda her schedule. Miranda looked at it with trepidation. All advanced-placement classes of course. And here was the locker number—again, by the gym! And the string of strange symbols that were already swimming before Miranda's eyes, just like in her nightmare. She rushed off—only fifteen minutes now to get her locker open and get to first period.

Miranda finally found her locker near some scary-looking utility room doors. The lockers at St. Philomena were huge, with double doors, like a church. Stuffing freshmen in them was so easy that nobody bothered. And instead of being a simple rectangle, all St. Philomena High lockers had an arch at the top. There was a carving of some kind of little monster right above Miranda's locker. He was sticking out his tongue.

Miranda set her new shoulder bag down and took a deep breath. She held her schedule up to peer at the combination in the dim light.

A scale was the first symbol. Not a good sign. She twirled the lock tentatively to the left until she found the scale. Crab—she twirled right slowly. What was this? She squinted. A bull? She turned the lock left. Crab again. Lion, fish—only one more left and maybe she'd get it open on the first try!

"*There* you are, Jellybean!" said a voice in her ear. Miranda screamed, and her hand slipped, spinning the lock wildly. She heard a *clunk* from behind the utility door and screamed again. Down the hall someone else screamed, too—probably making fun of her.

She turned to glare into the face of her boyfriend, Vincent. He was grinning and holding out a piece of paper and pen to her. He was wearing a strange skinny tie.

"You can be the first to sign up for the new Numismatic Club. You can even be the vice president if you want. I mean, I thought we'd vote on it, but who says it has to be a democracy?" said Vincent.

"You made me mess up my combination," Miranda muttered, looking at her schedule again to start over. "And that tie isn't dress code."

"Let me see," said Vincent, yanking it out of her hand. "Got it memorized yet? Mine's water guy, twins, fish, ram, virgin, crab, virgin."

Miranda ripped her schedule back out of his hand and scowled down at the lock as she murmured, "Scale. . . crab. . ."

"What's wrong with you?" Vincent asked.

"Shh—I'm concentrating . . ."

"You never wrote me back about the Numismatic Club in that letter I sent you last week from Chess Camp. Sorry I didn't text last night. We got back kind of late and my mom said I had to go to bed. But don't you think it'll get a lot of interest in the club signup today? I already found an advisor . . ."

Miranda tried to block out Vincent's chatter and the screams down the hall as she turned the lock. She came to the last symbol. She held her breath as she yanked on the locker handle. Nothing. She groaned and leaned her head on the locker door.

"Want me to do it?" Vincent asked, pushing her aside. "You sign up for Numismatic Club, and I'll open your locker."

"No!" Miranda pushed him back, putting her hand over the lock. "I have to figure it out. I can do this." She started again, trying to ignore Vincent's helpful suggestions.

Miranda was also trying to avoid talking about Numismatic Club, Vincent's fancy name for a bunch of geeks who liked coin collecting. When she first started dating Vincent, Miranda had pretended to be interested in coin collecting, too. But there was no way this year that she had time for his club. Just thinking about all the extracurriculars she had signed up for on top of her AP classes made Miranda anxious. She knew what her mom would say about Vincent's club. "You think this will impress a good school?"

The two-minute warning bell rang. Miranda yelped and yanked on her locker handle. Nothing. She finally let Vincent open the locker for her and dumped her lunch and coat inside. Her bag was already heavy, and she hadn't even gotten books. She took everything else with her anyway.

As Miranda sprinted up three flights of stairs to chemistry class, Vincent kept pace with her, talking the whole time. Neither noticed what was flying overhead. Or the banging on the lockers they passed. They made it through the chemistry classroom door just as the bell rang. The teacher looked up and sneered.

"I expect everyone to be in their seats when that bell rings," he said. Miranda quickly sat down in the nearest seat. Then she realized that she wasn't sitting in the front row as she always did. The year wasn't off to a good start.

The tardy bell had just sounded. Principal Jones was itching to get some paperwork done, but he didn't want to interrupt Dr. Spangler. Spangler was still going on about the architectural significance of St. Philomena High, blah blah. Why Principal Jones couldn't possibly put a new roof on the school unless he bought very expensive antique tiles like the originals, blah blah.

"Ivor Shandor was an unappreciated genius!" Spangler said, waving his arms. "If you'd read the authoritative biography I wrote about him, you'd know that he imported those slate tiles from Moldova. And you want to replace them with asphalt shingles!?"

"The roof is leaking," Jones said again, trying to be patient. "And parents are not going to like it if I raise tuition to buy imported roof tiles. I barely have enough in the budget to—"

"Mr. Jones!" the secretary banged open the door. "We need you to—" she broke off with a scream and fell to the floor, covering her head. Jones saw something dark flash past the door of his office.

"What in the world!?" Jones asked, trying to help up the secretary so he could get into the outer office.

"BATS!!" screamed the secretary, refusing to get off the floor. Jones gave up and stepped over her to get out the door. Spangler was right behind him.

Jones looked around wildly. Isaiah, the student office aide, was still at the copy machine, calmly making copies. Jones couldn't see anything wrong.

"Isaiah?" he asked.

Without looking up, Isaiah pointed to the window curtains.

Jones rushed over and shook the curtains. A bat burst out and flew across the room, disappearing behind a filing cabinet. The secretary screamed again.

"Please, stop that!" Jones barked. "It's just a poor confused animal. Isaiah, call one of the custodians."

"Can't," said Isaiah, rapidly pushing buttons on the copier. *Beep beep beeeep.*

"Oh really?" said Jones, getting steamed. "Just what—"

"They're all in the basement."

"So?"

"Dealing with the other bats."

"Other bats?" Jones moved to the other side of the copier, thinking he'd misheard.

Isaiah shrugged. "That's what I heard, anyway." He finally looked up at Jones. "That's where they came out."

Jones stared at him for a moment. Then he dashed out of the office. In the hall, he nearly collided with a teacher and student.

"Sorry," he said, trying to move around them.

"Mr. Jones!" the teacher grabbed his arm. "There are—"

"I know, I know," he said, impatiently, trying to shake the guy off. "I'm on my way—"

"Is the nurse here today? Where's the first-aid kit? Maybe we should call 911, they could be rabid—" the teacher babbled. Jones finally looked at him and the student next to him. Both had bloody gashes on their faces. Bites?

"You'd better stay here and deal with them," said a voice in Jones' ear. He spun around to see Spangler at his elbow. "I'll go see what's happening in the basement. I might be able to help with some little mysteries of the building." Spangler strode off. "Don't worry, Mr. Jones," he said over his shoulder.

Principal Jones didn't have long to wonder what Dr. Spangler was talking about. Screams and metallic pounding rang out from the nearby music wing. He dashed down the hallway and turned right, expecting to see dozens of screaming teenagers kicking their lockers. Instead the hallway was eerily empty.

The lockers were shaking. Students were kicking them—from inside. Every single locker seemed to have trapped its owner.

Jones ran to the first locker and screamed

through the grate, "What's your combination?"

The boy in the locker yelled, "Skull, dagger, unicorn, serpent, rhombus, rhombus, rhino." Or so Jones thought. He couldn't be certain, because the girl in the next locker desperately shouted "Crab, lion, scorpion, lion, ram, fish, bull!" Everybody was screaming his or her combination.

Jones clenched his teeth and tried the combination he thought he heard. He whispered under his breath, "Left *twins*, right *ram*, left *lion*, right *fish*, left *scorpion*, right *ram*, left all the way around and *virgin*. . ." He pulled up on the latch—and the whole lock came off in his hand. He stared at it for a moment before the whole locker slid down and disappeared into the floor. Jones stared down the hole in horror as it echoed with the scream of whoever had been in the locker.

Jones dropped the lock and staggered back from the opening in the bank of lockers. Had the wrong combination made it drop? Or the right one?

Principal Jones thought of himself as a man who didn't shock easily. He'd come to St. Philomena after twenty years as an assistant principal at St. Perdita's School for Wayward Boys in the next county. St. Philomena was supposed to be a piece of cake—no metal detectors, no bomb threats. Just an old Catholic high school in a sleepy little town.

"Piece of cake." He'd said those very words to himself when he took the job, and he was whispering them to himself again as he stared at the hole where that locker should have been.

His shock fading, he noticed another person in the hallway with him. She had her ear pressed against the locker grate, straining to hear the person inside. She began to turn the knob.

Jones jumped across the hall, slapping her hand away before she could pull the latch. The girl—her face showing signs of claw marks—was clearly scared out of her wits.

At that moment, Spangler burst into the hallway. He was completely white as he stammered at Jones and the terrified freshman. "Whatever you do," Spangler said, "don't try to open one of those lockers."

Pec, pec, delt, delt, bicep, bicep. Pec, pec, delt, delt, bicep, bicep. Dante's solo weight session was over. And since his first period was TAing for Coach Mick, he was indulging in a long shower. Coach barely noticed if he showed up. Dante didn't worry that anyone would notice him admiring his muscles because he hadn't seen anyone else this morning.

The guys' shower was one huge chamber. It was covered in tile, just like the rest of the basement, and its arched ceiling made for a deafening echo.

Glut, glut, quad, quad, calf, calf. Glut, glut, quad, quad, calf— CLICK. Though his eyes were closed, Dante sensed that the lights had gone out. Then his shower faded to a trickle and was gone.

"Aw, man. Whoever's out there better cut that junk out." Dante yelled.

As the echo faded, all he could hear in the locker room was the popping of soap bubbles in his unrinsed hair. No muffled laughter from any of the guys. No sound of high fives. He was certain that there was no one else in the locker room.

He worked his way along the shower wall until he found the entrance and the towel he'd left there. He got as much of the soap off as he could and opened his eyes. It made no difference at all. Not even the exit signs were on.

Dante wrapped the towel—which suddenly felt very small and thin—around his waist and began moving toward the lockers.

Finally he felt the first bumpy vents of a locker. Dante sighed in relief. He was getting really cold and couldn't wait to put on some clothes. And some underwear. He didn't like being naked and not knowing what else could be in the room with him.

Dante suddenly realized, though, that he didn't know exactly which gym locker belonged to him. It was 208, kind of in the middle in of the room. He tried to feel the numbers on the little plate on the locker in front of him, but he wasn't confident he could really tell what they were. Dante felt along the lockers until he thought he might have gone far enough. He began opening lockers and feeling inside to see if he could find his clothes. Some of the lockers did have things in them, but nothing that felt like his stuff.

While opening the tenth locker, Dante heard a faraway, drawn-out scream, a long whoosh, and a hollow bang. Then the same again. Again. Then silence. He heard his breath. He felt a rumbling under his feet. He held on tight to the locker door. The rumbling stopped.

Suddenly Dante couldn't stand being alone there in the dark any longer. He put his hand in the locker in front of him. Slippery fabric, like a pair of shorts. He grabbed them.

Whatever was on the hook under the shorts felt like a T-shirt, so he grabbed that too. He stuck one leg in the shorts and then the other, getting tangled up for a minute in his hurry. When he pulled them up they felt shorter and tighter than he expected, especially without boxers on.

What and whose are these? he wondered as he yanked the T-shirt on. It was tight too, and it didn't come down very far. Dante heard a clang echo from the shower area and froze. When he didn't hear anything more, he began feeling his way along the lockers toward the door to the hallway. He tried to be quiet, but mostly he just wanted to get out.

Dante felt his way around the corner and along the wall, where he fumbled for the door handle. He ripped it open and ran out into the hallway. Safe!

He blinked in the fluorescent light. It was quiet. He felt a bit silly. A draft of cold air from the locker room made him look down. He was wearing bright orange running shorts, two sizes too small, and a St. Philomena track T-shirt that barely came to the top of the shorts. (He noticed his muscles looked good in the tight shirt, though.)

Hearing steps down the hall, Dante looked up. He couldn't see who it was, but it looked like it might be one of the guys on the team. Dante panicked—he didn't want to explain how scared he'd been and how he ended up in these stupid clothes. It was probably just a circuit that overloaded or something.

He stepped back into the locker room, waiting for whoever it was to walk past. Meanwhile he tried the light switch. Nothing. He was listening hard for footsteps, so he jumped when the rumbling and cracking noises began again in the locker room, louder than before. A blast of cold air made all the hairs on his body stand up.

Dante threw open the door and ran back into the hallway. He looked for someone to tell, no matter how dumb he looked in these clothes. But the hallway was deserted.

He hesitated, looking around. Then he heard another yell directly overhead. He sprinted for the stairs.

At the tardy bell, the chemistry teacher stalked past Miranda. He locked the classroom door.

"I always lock the door after that bell," he informed them. "Anyone who isn't in his seat by the first bell will only receive half the points for any assignment turned in that day." Miranda was sure he glared at her. "Anyone who comes after the tardy bell shouldn't even bother coming. He won't be able to get in. Anyone want to leave now? The door's only locked from the outside."

The class was silent as he stared at all of them.

"Fine. Let's get started and see if you know anything useful." He began writing on the board. Everyone picked up their pens.

A loud rattling of the door handle caused everyone to look over. Outside the room, somebody pounded on the door. The teacher just shook his head and kept writing. Miranda thought she could hear the person yelling, "It's me, Jones! Open up!"

What did that mean? she wondered as she began copying formulas. The person kept pounding and rattling the door handle until the teacher walked over and clipped a wire to the handle on the inside. He flipped a switch on a box sitting on the counter next to the door.

"Aaaarghhhhhh!" everyone heard from outside the door. And then nothing.

"I hope all of you know enough to realize these metal door handles conduct electricity quite nicely. Does anyone know the maximum voltage and amperage the human body can sustain without permanent injury?"

The teacher (who still hadn't introduced himself, Miranda realized) began explaining the lab for the day. "As was stated on your supply list, which you received in the mail two weeks ago, our first unit uses strontium. Due to cuts to my supply budget, you'll need to bring many of your own chemicals. I trust you all remembered to bring your two ounces of strontium. Anyone who has forgotten it will, of course, fail this first unit."

Everyone, including Miranda, began to dig around in their bags. Everyone except Vincent. He leaned over to Miranda, "We can share yours, right? My mom didn't get me any yet."

Miranda stopped feeling around in her bag and stared at him. "You don't have any?"

"Shh, keep your voice down. I'll probably have some tomorrow. We'll just start with yours."

"But—"

"Find a lab bench with your partner and begin with the instructions on the board," the teacher said over the noise. Vincent got up and pulled out stools at the nearest lab bench. Miranda was still feeling around in her bag. She started pulling things out. She was sure she'd packed the little vial of strontium last night.

The teacher was looking at her, so she grabbed her bag and hurried over to Vincent.

"Where is it?" he asked.

"I don't—" Miranda piled her pencil case, notebooks, calculator, and binder on the table. "I was sure—" Then it hit her as she stared at the bottom of her bag. She'd put the strontium in her jacket pocket. She had meant to switch it to her bag during the car ride to school. But then her dad had been reciting all the locker combinations he had while at St. Philomena High and she'd forgotten.

"I don't have it," she whispered, not believing what she'd done. Of course, any other teacher would give you a pass to go get it, especially on the first day. She stared at Vincent, who looked as panicked as she felt. "I left it in my jacket. Omigod, I'm going to fail, I'm going to fail . . ." Miranda put her head in her hands. She'd never gotten a zero on an assignment before, let alone a whole unit. This was so unfair. Did this teacher want to ruin her chances at getting into a good college?

"You're going to fail?" Vincent's voice cracked. "*I'm* going to fail, too—I was counting on you to be prepared, like always. We can't fail—we'll both be grounded forever! Just ask him for a pass—say you have to go to the bathroom and then go to your locker instead. Tell him you've got your period or something."

Miranda opened her mouth to protest when the room was silenced by a series of screams and loud bangs from the hallway. The students all looked at the teacher.

"Go on, go on, get going!" he snapped. "I don't care what shenanigans are going on in the hallway. In this class we don't waste time. Even if you think you see a nuclear bomb blow up outside the window, I'm not interested in questions about anything that doesn't relate to this class," he said, pounding the table. He turned to write on the board again.

Conversations started up again as students got out their notebooks and settled at their lab benches.

"Go ask," Vincent hissed. The classroom phone rang shrilly over the noise. The teacher let it ring five times, then threw the chalk angrily at the board and stalked over to answer it.

"No!" said Miranda. "He'll know I forgot it—he could ask to see my strontium before he gives me a pass. And I'm NOT telling him I'm menstruating. You can ask him for a pass yourself. You didn't even bring your strontium to school. It would be fairer if you failed than if I did."

The teacher slammed down the phone, muttering to himself. His eyes swept the students at the lab benches. Miranda and Vincent leaned together, trying to look busy.

"Well, let's hear your great ideas," Vincent whispered snarkily. The teacher stalked into the supply closet at the front of the room.

"I'll just leave now. You'll have to distract him and let me back in when I knock softly. Or maybe I can leave something in the door so it doesn't close completely," Miranda said desperately. She couldn't think of anything else. She started shoving all her stuff back in her bag.

"No, I'm coming, too," said Vincent. They could still hear the teacher moving stuff around in the closet. Vincent held up his hand as Miranda started to argue. "It'll be more obvious if only one of us is missing. We can get back into this room from the physics classroom next door—remember? They connect through the supply closet. Besides, you can't even get your locker open. C'mon, let's GO." He grabbed his bag, keeping his eye on the closet.

Miranda didn't like it, but there wasn't time to fight about it. She looked around. None of the students were paying attention to them. Trying to look like she was just going to sharpen a pencil, she hurried toward the door.

"Flip the switch!" Vincent said, still watching the closet. Miranda did and then touched the door handle quickly. No shock. She turned it quietly and slipped out. Vincent was right on her heels.

"We did it!" he crowed and leaned over to kiss her.

Miranda pulled away. She was still annoyed with him. Then a rumbling through the floor made her lose her balance. As she fell, she heard more screams down the hall and saw something fly past. Her head hit the floor, and everything went black.

In the library, Mrs. Konstantinos was completing her ritual for the first day of school. She had written the locker combinations on all the students' schedules. All the schedules had been collected, except for those belonging to the few stragglers who were probably outside smoking. Mrs. Konstantinos didn't even need to look at the names to know who those students were. Nothing escaped her.

She cracked each knuckle slowly. Rebecca, her first-hour student library aide, flinched.

Mrs. Konstantinos wheezed her creaky-door laugh.

"Your mother never liked that either," she remarked.

Rebecca wondered what the heck Mrs. Konstantinos was talking about. Could she even see Rebecca where she was shelving books on the other side of the bookcases?

Mrs. Konstantinos ran her hands lovingly over the cracked leather cover of the book. She took a key from around her neck and unlocked a small cabinet next to the desk. The book fit perfectly inside, and the door of the cabinet had a small hole to accommodate the chain. Mrs. Konstantinos wasn't taking any chances.

"These books need mending," she said to Rebecca, pointing to a stack of books on a cart. "And some are sadly defaced. See what you can do with them. I will be in the lavatory."

She retired to her spacious private bathroom, just behind the circulation desk. She selected a pipe from the rack and filled it with tobacco, then sat down on the edge of an antique chair to light it. Then she leaned back and put her feet up on the edge of the sink.

The best part of the day, she thought. Now was a time to think about that noise she'd heard earlier—

BOOM! A rumble shook the school. Mrs. Konstantinos sat up.

"Whaaat—?" More rumbles followed. Mrs. Konstantinos's extra set of porcelain false teeth skittered off the sink and shattered on the floor.

"Ivor!" Mrs. Konstantinos turned even paler than she already was. She burst out of the bathroom, pipe still in hand. Bats were fluttering across the ceiling of the library.

"Shoo!" snorted Mrs. Konstantinos. The bats took one look at her and fled.

Mr. Konstantinos smiled, pulled a black shawl over her shoulders, and followed the bats into the hallway.

Bats. They were definitely bats. The first few times something swooped inches above Dante's still-wet hair as he ran for the stairs, he'd told himself it was a very big moth. Now there could be no doubt.

As he turned onto the second flight of the stairs out of the basement, he ran directly into a wall of bats. If he'd felt naked in his tiny running shorts before, it was nothing compared to what he felt now. But he didn't slow down. Dante covered his face with his forearm, imagined the bats were an opposing offensive line, and barreled through.

At the top of the stairs the bats thinned out somewhat. Dante could see empty hallways on either side. Right would take him to the main entrance, so he took a step.

And then he couldn't see anything because the lights went out. Before he could panic (again), the lights snapped back on, and now the hallway to his right wasn't empty. An oddly familiar female silhouette was slowly walking toward Dante. He instinctively stepped back. He prepared to turn in the other direction. Then the lights snapped out again. Dante stopped dead.

This time the lights stayed out. As Dante's eyes adjusted to the light, he could see the occasional bat circling in the gloom. He couldn't see the woman, so he was pretty sure she hadn't seen him. He wanted it to stay that way. Something was very wrong.

And over the sound of the bats' flapping and screeching, he heard something else. A clicking of shoes. A combination lock spinning. The clicking of a latch. And then *whoosh*, the sound of falling. A few more footsteps, and then another combination spun.

Dante pressed himself against the bank of lockers behind him.

"Get me out of here!" came the terrified whisper through the locker vent inches from his ear. "Please, just get me out of here. I'll do anything."

Dante jumped halfway across the hall. "Mother of—" He clapped his hand over his mouth just in time to hear another click and *whoosh!* And this time the whoosh came with a scream.

The lights clicked on again. Dante saw that the woman was Mrs. Konstantinos, the librarian. She turned toward him, placed her finger to her lips, and whispered, "Shhhhh."

Dante was in a full-on sprint when she turned back to the locker. He couldn't hear her whispering to herself, "Soon, Ivor. Very soon we will be rid of all these filthy children, and the world will know how right you were."

Click. *Whoosh.* Scream.

W hen Miranda opened her eyes, all she could see was Vincent's face. His breath smelled like spicy Cheetos, and it was making her nauseous. Or maybe that was the giant lump on the back of her head.

"I have a concussion," she moaned.

"C'mon, get up. We have to get going before he notices we're gone," said Vincent anxiously.

"People with concussions are supposed to lie still," Miranda murmured, closing her eyes again.

"Miranda. Harvard, Yale, Princeton, Tufts—these mean anything to you? Get up!"

"I'd never go to Tufts," Miranda snapped, opening her eyes. "Please. OK, what happened?" Miranda got to her feet slowly. Vincent tugged on her arm.

"Dunno. There was this weird shaking and you fell." Vincent started jogging down the hall. Miranda tried to keep up, her bag banging on her hip and her head throbbing.

"But I heard screaming," she said breathlessly as they passed closed classroom doors. "And I think I saw something, too."

"You said yourself you have a concussion," said Vincent over his shoulder. "Just hallucinations."

"You really think I have a concussion?" Miranda said, alarmed. "Wait up! My bag is heavy!"

Vincent paused and grabbed her bag, slinging it over his shoulder on top of his own.

"I did hear some screaming, but that's hardly strange. Like the chemistry teacher said, just kids messing around in the hallway."

"But—" Miranda's words died as they

rounded the corner to the stairs. Across from the stairs, where a row of lockers used to be, was a giant hole in the wall.

"What's that?" said Miranda. Vincent looked but didn't break stride. He pulled open the door to the stairs.

"Maybe they're doing construction or something on those. C'mon."

Miranda hesitated.

"Harvard, Yale—"

"Shut up," she said, following him down the stairs. Through the window to the first floor, she saw another hole where lockers used to be.

"Vincent, look! Another one! That's too weird—maybe we should tell someone."

"Your locker's in the basement. We're almost there!"

"You can go ahead if you want. The office is right here. I'm just going to ask the secretary about it." Miranda went into the hallway and across to the school office. Vincent trailed after her, huffing to himself.

Miranda stepped into the office and said to the back of the secretary's head, "Umm, I'm out of class on a bathroom pass, but I noticed that there are some lockers missing and—"

"Save your breath," said a guy on the other side of the office, by the copy machine. "She fainted."

"What?" Miranda said.

"Because of the bats."

"Bats?!" Miranda squeaked. Vincent looked around nervously.

"They're gone now," said the kid impatiently. "But look at this, man. The copier just keeps spitting out these symbols, no matter what I do."

He handed a piece of paper to Miranda.

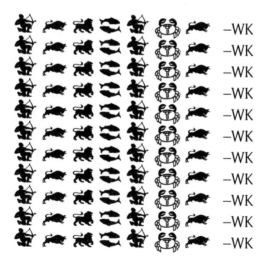

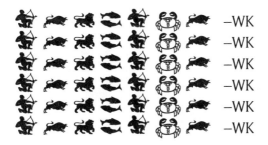

"I mean, there's nothing even on the glass," the kid stared down at it. "It's *awesome*."

"There's no one here to tell," said Vincent, tugging on Miranda's arm as she stuffed the paper in her pocket. "Let's go."

"Well, you should wipe her face with cold water. And can you tell her or someone about the lockers?" said Miranda as Vincent pulled her out the door. The copier kid didn't respond—he was too busy gazing at the symbols.

"That was odd," said Miranda, "maybe we should—"

But Vincent was already in the stairwell, heading for the basement. Miranda sighed and followed.

As Dante jogged down the hall toward the back doors of the school, he noticed how strangely quiet it was. *Where is everyone?* he wondered. When he reached the doors, he threw himself against the closest one. It was locked. He pushed on the next door handle—locked.

Sometimes only one is unlocked, he thought frantically. He pushed at the next set of double doors. Nothing. He tried all four doors again, slamming his weight against the metal bars.

They wouldn't budge. He started to look around for something he could use to break the glass.

He thought he could still hear the librarian in the hallway around the corner. Part of him felt like he should want to go back. To try and stop whatever crazy thing she was doing and save anyone she was hurting. Part of him argued he had to find someone to tell. And all of him just wanted to get OUT!

And once I'm out I can get help—there's no one here, he thought as he paced around, looking for something he could pick up and swing.

Then he noticed the junior varsity trophy case. If he could get in there, he might be able to break the door glass with a trophy. He wondered if any of the trophies were heavy enough. As he circled the case, he noticed there were a lot more certificates than trophies anyway.

Dante heard running footsteps behind him and spun around, fists up.

A pasty-looking old guy jogged toward him. His mouth was open. He gasped for breath. His shirt had come untucked, and his tie flapped.

That guy looks like he's about to have a heart attack, Dante thought, watching him warily.

"You!" gasped the man. "Come with me—I think I know how stop—but I'll need—" He stopped and bent over, coughing. Dante could hardly understand him. He couldn't tell if it was because the man was out of breath or had a strange accent.

"Come where?" Dante asked, suspicious.

"Basement," the man panted, gesturing back the way Dante had come.

"Nuh-uh," said Dante emphatically. "I ain't going back down there! We got to tell someone—there's bats or something, and then the librarian lady is, like, making the lockers disappear and I heard screaming and—"

"I know, I know," said the man, finally getting his breath back. "I think I can stop it. But I have to have some help, and everyone seems to have disappeared. I'm afraid they're all trapped. Now come along before something worse happens!" He grabbed Dante's arm and started pulling him down the hall.

"But that's where *she* is!" said Dante, pulling back and stopping the man in his tracks. This out-of-shape guy was no match for Dante's strength.

"We'll just have to risk it—that's the fastest way to the basement from here. Now stop arguing and wasting time! Young people in America are so difficult," the man said. He charged on down the hall. "Or maybe you're just frightened," he threw over his shoulder.

"I'm not scared," snarled Dante as he caught up in a few strides. "Who said I'm scared?"

As they approached the corner, Dante pulled the man back. "She's down there," he hissed.

They listened for a moment. The guy peeked around the corner.

"AAAARRGHHH!" he screamed, jumping back, knocking into Dante.

"Well, well," said Mrs. Konstantinos, gliding around the corner. "If it isn't the great Dr. Spangler. This is not a good time for a sniveling little coward like you to be out and about." She paused. "You know, Dr. Spangler, I read your so-called biography of my Ivor." She stared at him for a moment. "Trash!" she hissed. "That's what I think of it. I keep it in my bathroom to use as

TOILET PAPER," she shrieked.

Whoa, that lady is messed up, thought Dante, backing up.

"Ex . . . excuse me?" blinked Dr. Spangler. "What, ma'am, are you talking about?"

"The things you wrote about my Ivor's visions! You dismissed them as *a family strain of mental illness—*" Mrs. Konstantinos was breathing heavily now.

"It's well documented in my book that Ivor Shandor's parents were both—" Dr. Spangler sounded huffy now.

"And such sloppy research! The footnote on page 145 is entirely off-base! What do you have to say about that, Dr. Spangler?" Mrs. Konstantinos looked triumphant.

"Wait, are you sure about the footnote? I caught that mistake as well, but my editor assured me it would be fixed—dear, dear," Dr. Spangler shook his head.

They're both crazy, decided Dante as he began to inch away.

"But what exactly is your connection with Ivor Shandor, ma'am? Surely you are too young to have—"

Mrs. Konstantinos let out a wild crackle that froze Dante in his tracks.

"There is so much you don't know, Dr. Spangler, especially for one who claims to be the expert on Ivor Shandor. Well, you shall see soon enough just what a genius Ivor is and how real his visions are. Now, if you'll excuse me, I have work to do."

Mrs. Konstantinos walked to the next set of lockers. She spun the lock rapidly back and forth while Dante and Dr. Spangler watched as though hypnotized. She pulled on the locker handle, and the rest of the locker dropped away.

"Stop—you can't—" Spangler tried to get between Mrs. Konstantinos and the next locker, but she pushed him away impatiently.

"Go away, doctor, and do whatever it is you think you can do. And Dante," she looked at him over her glasses. "I don't think those . . . clothes meet the dress code. And you'll want to be properly attired for what will occur soon." She cackled again, pulled on the locker handle, and watched the locker disappear with satisfaction. They all heard a faint scream from below.

Dr. Spangler grabbed Dante's arm and pulled him toward the basement stairs. Dante didn't resist.

Miranda almost ran right into Vincent at the bottom of the stairs. He had stopped abruptly.

"What—ohhh . . ." she said, peering around him into the dark of the basement hallway.

They were quiet for a moment. Miranda thought she heard flapping.

"Remember how that kid said there were bats? I think I hear . . ."

"Shhh," said Vincent. They could hear someone walking, and then they could see a light wavering at the end of the hallway.

"That must be a janitor," said Vincent, starting to walk slowly into the hall. "Must have blown a fuse or something down here. If we can borrow a flashlight or something, I can get your locker open and we can be back in class in minutes."

"I can open my own locker," Miranda muttered, reluctantly inching into the dark hallway. "Vincent, why don't you just use your cell-phone screen for light?"

"*Shhhhh!* Do you want to ruin everything? It's against the rules to have a cell phone on school property, and my mother said it was only for emergencies!"

Miranda threw up her hands. "This isn't an emergency?!"

The light was getting closer. "Hello?" Vincent called, feeling his way along the wall. "Uh, sir? Can we borrow a flashlight to get something really important from a locker? We have a pass from our AP Chemistry class—"

They heard talking. The footsteps quickened as the light bobbed toward them.

"Who goes there?" called a voice with a British accent. "I warn you, we're armed!"

"That's not the janitor," said Miranda, stopping. "Vincent, come back here!" She shuffled along the wall until she found Vincent. She grabbed his hand. The light and footsteps came closer as they held their breaths, uncertain what to expect.

"Is this some kind of joke?" Vincent murmured. "Did I miss it? Is it like Pretend You're British Day? Or Medieval Castle Day? I never remember to wear my pajamas on Pajama Day during homecoming week, but I can't believe I'd miss this . . ."

Soon they could see faces in the bobbing light. Miranda blinked. That was Dante Grant behind the man she didn't know. Dante looked so much bigger than she'd remembered. She'd known him since the beginning of elementary school, but they hadn't had a class together since middle-school gym. They probably hadn't talked since then, either. What was going on?

"Are you friend or foe?" the man demanded as the light from his lighter flame fell on Miranda and Vincent.

"Uh, friend, I think," said Vincent. "Care to tell us what's going on? We need to get something in my girlfriend's locker and get back to class."

Miranda saw that Dante recognized her. His eyes flicked to her again when Vincent said "girlfriend." In a split second Miranda remembered the Snoopy valentine Dante had given her when he was in fifth grade and she was in sixth. *Just a little hi from someone who's feeling kind of shy.* She'd always wondered if he was trying to say something or that was just a dumb joke. She shook her head to clear it. Dante looked at her again.

The man studied them carefully. "Are they friends?" he asked Dante finally.

"Uh, what?" Dante seemed surprised that someone had addressed him.

"Are they actually students? Do you know them? Or are they zombies or vampires masquerading as students?" the man said impatiently.

"Oh, yeah, I know them—that's Miranda and that's—" Dante paused. "Uh . . ."

"Vincent," said Vincent, annoyed. "President of the St. Philomena Numismatic Club."

"Oh, lovely," said the man, holding out

his hand to each of them. "Dr. Spangler. We must talk shop sometime—I have a little coin collection myself. But not now."

He was suddenly serious again. "You seem to be blissfully unaware, but there is danger afoot and my young companion and I are out to stop it. What did you say your name was again?" he asked, turning to Dante.

"Dante," Dante muttered, yanking on his shirt. Miranda squinted at him in the wavering light—what was he wearing?

"Very apt," said Dr. Spangler dreamily. Miranda raised her eyebrows at Dante. He shrugged but looked nervous.

"Now," said Dr. Spangler briskly. "The school seems to be attacking, or at least trapping, everyone. I have reason to believe from my extensive research on the architect, Ivor Shandor, that this is the result of a plan he put in place when the school was built one hundred years ago. Shandor was a genius, but he was also unbalanced. He believed he could bring about an occult occurrence with certain rituals. I did not until today realize that he connected these rituals to this school, but given all that's

happening and some things that woman said—"
he paused, frowning.

"Who?" asked Miranda.

"The librarian," said Dante.

"Mrs. Konstantinos? What does she have to
do—?"

"Duh," said Vincent. "She's perfect for the
part. *He vas my boyfriend!*" he yodeled, making
everyone jump.

"What's your problem, man?" Dante said
aggressively.

Vincent rolled his eyes. "*Jeepers*, Muscle
Man, guess you're not so familiar with the
works of Mel Brooks. I mean, it's obvious—"

Miranda put her hand over Vincent's
mouth. "Vincent!" She turned to Spangler.
"What do you mean, 'occult occurrence'?"

Spangler rubbed the back of his neck.
"Right, well, it's rather a long story and very
complicated. I'm not really sure there's time or
that you'd understand—"

"Hey, some of us are future Ivy Leaguers,"
said Vincent.

"One of us," muttered Miranda.

"Vincent's right." Everybody turned to

Dante. "Well, I don't know about the Ivy League crap, but you'd better tell us about Shandor. Something is seriously screwed up here, and this building isn't letting us out without a fight. So we better know what we're up against."

"Yes, I suppose I'd better explain," said Spangler. "But first, I wonder if we might find another source of illumination. This lighter isn't going to last forever." The flame was getting disturbingly low. "And those dreadful bats seem to be where the light isn't."

"Don't look at me," said Dante, gesturing to his clothing.

Miranda whacked Vincent across the chest again. "I think even your mom would call this an emergency. You can use your cell phone as a light."

"Wait, you've got a cell phone?" asked Dante. "Why don't you—I don't know—use it to call for help?!"

Without a word, Vincent pulled out the phone, but when he hit the power button, his face, bathed in green light, showed only confusion.

"What, no signal?"

"No anything," and he turned the screen toward the others. It pulsed in varying shades of green.

"Ivor, you were a genius." The flickering light of Spangler's lighter was replaced by the sickly green glow of Vincent's cell, which was now a very expensive flashlight. It was brighter, but hardly more comforting.

"So, tell us what's up with Shandor," said Dante.

"As it turns out, it wasn't chance that brought one of Europe's great architects to Bridgewater to build a high school," Spangler said. "It was geology."

"Rocks for jocks. Admissions counselors see right through that on a transcript."

"Shut up, Vincent!" Miranda hissed.

"As I was saying, it was geology that brought Shandor here. Specifically, a sinkhole that appeared in Bridgewater the year before Shandor dropped everything to come here and build a school. As I'm sure a future Ivy Leaguer must know, a sinkhole occurs when the stone underlying the surface suddenly collapses, creating a hole seemingly out of nowhere. The hole itself can be only a few meters deep. Or it can be thousands of meters."

"Let me guess," said Dante. "The one in Bridgewater is really deep." The pieces of the puzzle were coming together.

"Correct," said Spangler. "I believe it may be the deepest in North America, perhaps the world."

"But wait, I've never heard of a sinkhole in Bridgewater—"

"Is it—"

Miranda and Dante both started to talk at once and then both stopped to apologize to each other.

"No one has seen the Bridgewater sinkhole for a little more than a hundred years. Shandor arrived here shortly after it opened and within days had charmed the city officials into allowing him to donate his services as an architect for any building they wanted, as long as he could build it over the sinkhole and have complete control over the materials."

"But why would he want to build a school over a huge hole in the ground?" Vincent asked.

"He didn't care about the school. He would have built a roller rink if they'd asked him to. What the people of Bridgewater wanted the building for didn't matter. Shandor believed it would eventually serve a much darker purpose."

"Spit it out," exclaimed Dante.

"Shandor's specialty as an architect was entryways—grand doorways, entrance halls, gates, and the like. It's my belief that this school is an entryway of sorts. Though it's not really a front door—more of a trapdoor. A trapdoor over h—"

The building rocked and seemed to tilt steeply before righting itself.

The tremor lasted only moments, but it was
enough to knock Dante, Spangler, and Miranda
to the floor and to send Vincent reeling backward
against the bank of lockers. As he grabbed for
something to brace himself, his phone clattered to
the floor in front of him, face down.

Dante started. "Is everybody all ri—" He bit
off his question.

Click.

In the darkness, everyone's hearing seemed
to sharpen. In a flash, Dante dove for where

he thought the phone might be. He fumbled it right-side-up and looked up in time to see exactly why the St. Philomena lockers were so large.

As the latch moved, the large floor tile beneath the locker's owner tilted down violently, like a seesaw. The two locker doors swung apart with ridiculous force. With the locker wide open, the floor pitched forward, as though a huge weight had landed on the opposite side of the seesaw, launching the locker's owner—now the locker's victim—inside.

Vincent hadn't been standing directly in front of the locker. When the trap was sprung, only one foot had stood on the seesawing part of the floor. So instead of being driven with terrible force headfirst into the back of the locker as the other students must have been, Vincent was able to catch the side of the locker. His head still hit the back of the locker with a sickening *thud*.

With another mechanical click, the floor righted itself. The door began to swing back into place. Dante dove like he was the last defender going for a streaking wide receiver's ankles. He grabbed the edge of the nearest of the locker's doors. It stopped for a moment, but then Dante felt the tremendous power of whatever mechanism was closing the door. The door began to drag him. It had about eight inches to go before he'd have to let go and lose Vincent or risk losing his fingers (and probably Vincent too).

"Guys! A little help here!" screamed Dante.

Miranda and Spangler scrambled to grab the door. The three of them succeeded in pulling it back another few inches.

"Young man! Now would be a good time to—"

Miranda yelled over him, "Vincent! Fat envelope from Princeton!"

At that, Vincent heaved himself through the gap. He rolled clear just as Dante, Spangler, and Miranda let the door slam shut. The crash of the door echoed down the hall, disturbing the bats roosting just beyond the light of Vincent's phone.

"Well," said Vincent, "at least we know what happened to everyone else."

"Time is running out," Spangler hissed as they crouched on the floor. Miranda clung to Vincent's arm. "Listen carefully. I have what may be the key, but I need help interpreting it. I was doing a bit more research on Shandor in preparation for the next edition of my book. As I leafed through the blueprints and architectural notes in the school library, this sheet of paper fell out. Listen."

The testimony of Wassily Konstantinos, chief engineer for Ivor Shandor

I can scarcely bring myself to write these words, but I know I must. I know Master Shandor to be insane. If this building and its sinister purpose were not enough evidence, then what I saw today must leave me with no doubts.

I was checking the work of the bricklayers on the outer walls of the boiler room when I heard Shandor enter. He was not alone. With him was one of the apprentice pipe fitters—a lad of no more than sixteen, and small for that age. The master led him over near the edge of the Pit at the room's center. The floor was still unfinished over the sinkhole. He asked the boy to pick up a small, heavy crate. As the boy knelt to lift the load, the master stepped back, drew up his cane, and brought it down on the child's skull. It was a miracle I did not cry out in horror.

But the blow was not the end of the atrocity. The boy was motionless for only a

*moment while the master satisfied himself
that he was alone. As the boy attempted to
push himself onto his hands and knees, the
master placed his boot firmly on the wretch's
ribs. With one hard push he sent the boy
plummeting over into the terrible abyss.*

*The master peered over the edge for
a moment. Then he turned his attention
to the compass that he is never without
these days—though I cannot understand
why. With the iron ore deposits that line
the pit, the instrument's needle does
nothing more than spin.*

*Frighteningly, he seemed to take great
pleasure in what he saw on the compass.*

*Having seen this, I am resolved to do
whatever I can to hamper the master's
plan. I know I do not have the courage
to confront him, and outright sabotage
of the building's mechanism is out of the
question. He would know in an instant
that his creation had been marred.
What I can do is make subtle changes. I
can misalign critical parts of the locker
mechanisms—parts that I daresay I*

know better than he. The building will still work, but it will do so more slowly than the master intends, and I pray this may give those poor souls caught in its clutches the time to escape.

My dear wife does not know of my plan, and she must not. She believes in the master's vision with all her heart. I do not pretend she would take my side if forced to choose.

May God have mercy on my soul and hers,

W.K.

"So that's why Mrs. Konstantinos was spinning all those combos. She was undoing her husband's sabotage!" It chilled Dante to remember her methodically moving from locker to locker.

"But if that's our Mrs. Konstantinos's husband, wouldn't it make her," Miranda gulped, "like, over a hundred years old?"

Spangler sighed. "I don't understand it myself, but clearly she is mixed up in this in a bad way. This makes this document all the more important—"

"That document is trash—the ravings of a coward," came a cold voice from just beyond the light of Vincent's phone. Then came the sound of a match striking, and a candle flickered to life. Mrs. Konstantinos stared at the four with complete contempt. "My husband was a fool. Every moment I have lived since that day has been to prove to the master that *I* never lost faith in his genius. My husband disappointed the master, but I never will." Her free hand disappeared into her shawl and came out with what was unmistakably a gun—a very old gun, but still a gun. "I won't have you ruining things now."

Dante, who had been seated near the middle of the hallway, edged back from the candle's light. He cast a quick sideways glance at Vincent, who seemed to understand. Dante slid closer to Miranda, whose eyes were locked on Mrs. Konstantinos.

"Mrs. Konstantinos, look, I'm really sorry about those overdue books," said Vincent. Dante eased off one of Miranda's shoes, hoping she'd catch on and not make a sound. Vincent continued, "I swear, I'll return—"

"Silence, fool," she said. She cocked the gun. "It would mean nothing to me to destroy you."

"Come on, will that gun even fire? I mean it looks even older than—"

Everything happened very quickly, and nobody was sure what came first. Dante definitely threw Miranda's shoe. Vincent definitely dropped his phone facedown. And Mrs. Konstantinos definitely dropped her candle and fired her pistol—which definitely worked.

And then the building took over again. It seemed like the whole floor dropped six inches and then stopped just as suddenly. The ceiling didn't hold up well under the strain, and its massive tiles began to crumble.

"Is everyone all right?" asked Miranda, still in darkness. "Vincent?! Say something!"

Everyone held their breaths for what seemed like forever. "Sorry, I was just enjoying everyone's concern," Vincent said. He flipped on his phone's screen again.

Mrs. Konstantinos lay unmoving, a large chunk of ceiling tile and Miranda's left shoe near her head.

"Nice throw," said Spangler.

"Is she . . . dead?" asked Dante.

Miranda scrambled over and searched for a pulse under the high neck of the librarian's dress. "No, I think she just hit her head." Miranda grabbed her shoe and the gun.

"Careful with that thing," winced Spangler.

"Relax," she said as she spun the cylinder on the ancient revolver. "Firearms safety merit badge, eighth grade. Besides, looks like she only had one bullet." Miranda flung the gun aside and pulled on her shoe. "What now?"

"Look, we have to get to the boiler room. There's no other way. Why Shandor was throwing people into the sinkhole, I don't want to imagine. But note how Wassily Konstantinos says they were in the boiler room." He gestured to the paper again. "And your dear librarian clearly didn't want us heading in that direction." He pointed at the concussed Mrs. Konstantinos. "I believe some crucial part of the mechanism must lie there. But I'm not sure we should go into that room unprepared . . ."

"I thought you said you were armed," said Vincent.

"Ah, that was merely to frighten you. Before I knew if you were friend or foe . . ." said Spangler.

They all looked around and at each other as though helpful items might suddenly appear. Dante tugged on his shorts and shirt.

"Don't look at me," he said sourly. "It's not like I'm hiding some sticks of dynamite on me."

Vincent snapped his fingers.

"I've got it. I'll be right back." Vincent flipped open his cell and followed the faint green beam down the hall.

"Vincent!" yelled Miranda.

"I say, what's he up to?" said Spangler.

He stopped about thirty lockers away and yelled "Here it is. Jellybean, what's your combo again?"

Dante's eyes widened.

"Just kidding, I already memorized it for y—"

Dante sprinted down the hall toward Vincent. In seconds he had him wrapped up and sprawling on the floor like a JV running back. Vincent looked up, stunned. "Don't try the locks, man," Dante said.

Vincent was gasping from the impact, but he managed to cough and point at the bottom of the locker. Miranda's scarf was jammed in the door. The locker wasn't latched.

"Uhh, thanks man, but I'm not *that* dumb," wheezed Vincent, massaging his chest. "I was just teasing Miranda. You know, she never locks her locker because she can't remember or do the combination. She won't admit it, of course. She has to be perfect at everything. But I saw her shove the scarf in the door this morning. She had that same scarf stuck in the corner all last year just to keep her locker open."

Dante looked confused. Miranda buried her face in her hands, glad no one could see her in the dark.

"But anyway," continued Vincent, "Miranda does have a weapon, of sorts, in her locker. It's why we were coming here in the first place."

Spangler spoke impatiently. "Well, what is it?"

"Is the suspense killing you?" said Vincent, grinning. "First, let's make sure I can get it without being eaten by a giant kangaroo or something."

He approached the locker carefully, his legs braced wide over the trick floor. With one finger he tugged on the door on the locker. Everyone held their breaths. Vincent stuck all his fingers in the space where the scarf jammed the locker and pulled.

The floor stayed put. The door swung open. Everyone let out a breath in relief.

Vincent stuck his hand into the locker and began rummaging through Miranda's coat.

"Aha," he said, turning away from the locker and walking back to Spangler and Miranda. Dante followed. Vincent opened his hand to reveal a small vial.

"What's this?" asked Spangler, annoyed with Vincent's melodrama.

"Oh, just a little powdered strontium," said Vincent casually. "You know, the stuff that will spontaneously ignite when exposed to the air at room temperature. Could come in handy."

"Hmph," said Spangler. "I guess we'll see about that. Let's go to the boiler room." He took Vincent's phone and began walking down the hall. "Judging by the blueprints, it should be around here. Every other time I visited the school, it was always locked. I could never find anyone with a key, so I've never actually been inside."

"I have," said Dante, surprising everyone. They all looked at him. "For football," Dante explained. Miranda raised her eyebrows. "Just a little joke," said Dante. Everyone kept looking at him, but he didn't say any more.

"Right," said Spangler finally. "Very helpful." He stopped in front of a metal door painted black. "I think this is it—do you agree?" he asked Dante.

Dante shrugged. "Dunno, I was blindfolded," he replied.

"Ahh, I see," said Spangler. He pulled cautiously on the door handle. Everyone else backed away. Nothing happened. Spangler jiggled the handle and pulled harder. Nothing. He muttered to himself, examining the handle from all angles.

Vincent looked at his watch and murmured to Miranda, "Maybe we should just go back to class—I think this guy might be a nut."

BOOM! An explosion rocked the floor under their feet. They all stumbled into each other. In the quiet afterward, they could hear what sounded like rocks falling in the boiler room.

Spangler looked panicked. "Look, I have an idea of what Shandor was trying to do. He had many . . . *odd* ideas. I believe he wanted to bring the world to an end, and that he thought he might be able to do it by means of—"

The floor jolted again.

"Spit it out!" screamed Miranda.

"By dropping a building full of people into the sinkhole! A massive human sacrifice to change the electromagnetic forces of the Earth!"

Vincent, Miranda, and Dante looked horrified.
    "So that's where everybody went when
their lockers dropped?" Dante could barely get
out the words.

    "Not necessarily," replied Spangler. "It's
possible they're all in a chamber beneath the
basement. Shandor would have counted on
dropping everyone all at once bring about the,
uh, desired result."

    "So let's get to the boiler room before
this mechanism thing finally does what it's

supposed to," said Vincent.

"We'll have to break down the door to get in."

Everyone looked at Dante. He was the muscle, after all. But Dante shook his head.

"Young man, don't you understand what's at stake?!" Spangler shrieked.

"There's another way in," Dante said. Vincent started laughing.

"Why didn't you say that before?" demanded Spangler testily.

Dante shrugged. "You didn't ask."

"Well, lead on, lead on," said Spangler, irritated.

Dante led them back toward the locker rooms. As Dante pushed open the door, Miranda cleared her throat.

"Uh, Dante? This is the girls' locker room."

"I know," said Dante. "Trust me."

Inside it was just as pitch black as the hallway. Occasionally they could hear the loud echo of a drip splashing on the floor.

"I think it's this way," whispered Dante, taking the phone from Vincent. "Wasn't this thing a lot brighter before?"

"The battery's going," said Vincent. "Can you hurry up, man? I dimmed the light to save the battery a little. Or maybe you could just get us there in the dark so we can save some juice?"

Dante muttered something and shut off the screen.

"We better stick together," he said quietly, grabbing Miranda's hand and beginning to feel his way forward again. Vincent grabbed her other arm.

"Children, where are you?" said Spangler from behind them. Dante paused as they listened to Spangler shuffling closer.

"Ow," said Vincent, "That's my—"

"Shut up," growled Dante, pulling them all forward again.

It seemed like forever, but it was probably only a few minutes before Dante breathed, "This is it, I think."

He gave Miranda's hand a little squeeze and then let go. They all heard something clang down around their knees. Dante grunted, and then there was a screech of metal and a louder clang.

"Got it," said Dante.

"What is it?" whispered Miranda.

"Vent. It's a bit of squeeze—I'll go first," said Dante.

"OK," he said a moment later, his voice coming from the other side.

Miranda ran her hands down the wall until she felt the opening. She put her hands on the sides and stuck her head into the hole. She put her hands out to feel the floor and then crawled awkwardly through. Dante fumbled in the dark to find her arm and pull her over to the side. Vincent came through next, then Spangler.

"I think we'd better see what we have," said Spangler, attempting to sound calm. The room was eerily quiet. Were they even in the boiler room?

There was rustling as Dante attempted to hand Spangler the phone. Suddenly he didn't want to be the one to turn on a light.

Spangler turned on the screen. He held the phone up high. They all looked around, but they couldn't see much more than the wall they'd just climbed through. Then the light went out.

"**H**ave no fear, strontium's here!" said Vincent cheerily.

"If you have some kind of plan, we'd all like to hear it," said Spangler, sounding irritated.

"Well, I haven't been lugging these bags around this whole time for nothing," said Vincent. "They're full of lovely combustibles. At least Miranda's is, since she has a three-subject college-ruled notebook for each class. Let's see if we can get a nice little fire going here." They could hear him ripping and crumpling paper.

"Vincent, what are you doing?" cried Miranda.

"Well, we're not going to be able to do anything unless we can see. You can sacrifice one, maybe two notebooks for a good cause, can't you?" said Vincent, continuing to rip and crumple.

"That's not what I mean—we don't even know what the strontium will do. If it's safe, or—"

"He's right, though," said Dante, finding Miranda's hand again and giving it another squeeze. "We gotta have light."

"OK, here goes!" said Vincent. Everyone heard a faint pop and saw a little flash in the glass vial. Then nothing.

"Stupid chemistry book—made this stuff sound so fabulously dangerous," he muttered.

"If we have to build a bonfire from my notebooks," said Miranda icily, "Why don't we just use Dr. Spangler's lighter?"

"Oh yeah," said the guys.

Spangler fumbled in his pockets. "I'm not sure there is any fuel left—it was quite low— where are those notebooks?"

"Oh, give it to me," snapped Miranda.

"Right, you were in Girl Scouts," muttered Vincent.

"I'll let you know as soon as I find any rare coins that need to be identified, OK?" Everyone heard the scratch of the lighter wheel, and then the flame lit up Miranda's face. She bent over the pile of crumpled papers.

"Move our bags back," she ordered. "And you all better start looking around for something else to burn, because this paper won't last long. And I don't actually have that many notebooks in my bag."

The notebook paper flared up brightly as Miranda expertly fed the fire with strips of the notebook covers.

"Hurry up!" she said. Everyone scrambled around, looking on the floor. Spangler threw a handful of dried leaves from a corner on the fire.

"Here are a few wood scraps," said Vincent eagerly, about to drop them on the fire. "Stop!" screamed Miranda. "The fire's not hot enough to burn those. They'll just crush it." She looked around wildly. "Dante, give me your T-shirt, quick."

Dante whipped it off and handed it to her, then tried not to feel self-conscious.

"Want mine, too?" said Vincent, starting to unbutton it.

"No," Miranda murmured. Dante's shirt caught fire and burned merrily. She held a piece of wood to the fire and watched it lick the edges. When it finally caught fire, everyone cheered. Miranda gave a small smile as she dropped the wood on top of the burning shirt.

"We'll be OK for a little bit now for light," said Miranda.

Everyone turned to look around the room.

The feeling of that boiler room tile on his bare feet brought Dante back to his freshman initiation. At least he wasn't naked this time. Almost, but not quite. And there was some light from the fire. Of course, the building might drop itself into a bottomless pit at any moment. But you couldn't have everything.

It had been several minutes since the last shock, and it was hard to concentrate. But Dante and the others were listening for all they were worth. Where was the mechanism that must be controlling the process?

"I believe that the mechanism is designed to make the building fold in on itself. When it reaches a certain point, that is, the building will swing apart like two sides of a trapdoor and drop itself and everyone in it into the pit," Spangler had explained.

The thought was too horrible for Vincent to make a lame joke. And Dante saw no way to muscle through the danger. Only Miranda seemed to keep it together.

"We've got to divide up and find the mechanism," she'd said. "It must make some kind of noise. I think the fire's going well enough that I can help. We'll each take a quarter of the room. Keep your ears open. Yell when you find something."

Dante had started at the outer edge of his quarter, and so far he was halfway to the center. All he could hear was the sound of his sweaty feet as they stuck slightly to the smooth tiles. He didn't have any idea what he was looking for.

He glanced across the room at Miranda, over by the fire. She was feeling her way along the wall, her eyes half closed. Dante stared at her—the way the light flickered over her face—

Hiss. Miranda disappeared as the room was plunged into darkness. Vincent started screaming.

"Vincent, shut up!!" Miranda yelled. "Let me see—or feel—something wet fell on the fire. All the paper and wood is wet but maybe . . . does the lighter still work?"

There was scratching sound and little flare. For a second they saw the gleam of Spangler's glasses. Then nothing. More scratching.

"I'm sorry," said Spangler wearily. "The fuel's all gone."

Everyone was silent. Dante slumped on the floor. He just didn't feel like standing anymore. This was it. He was going to die in these stupid shorts and never get to play varsity.

Then he felt a thrumming under his hand. He put his ear down on the floor. He could hear a series of metallic clicks and feel vibrations.

"I . . . I think I found something!" he said.

"Great timing," he heard Vincent mutter.

"No, come over here—I can feel it vibrating. And if I put my ear down, I can hear it clicking.

Wait, I think I can feel a crack—" He started to feel around the tiles on the floor.

"Where are you?" Vincent, Spangler, and Miranda all cried at once.

"Oh, uh, kind of toward the middle," said Dante, straining his eyes in the dark. He could hear shuffling noises but couldn't see a thing.

"You have to keep talking," said Miranda. "This room is huge. It's really hard to keep my sense of direction."

"OK, I'm right here," said Dante.

"Keep talking!" they all yelled, not sounding much closer than before.

"Um," said Dante. He couldn't think of anything to say. Test, test, one, two?

"Could you at least hum?" said Vincent, sarcastically.

Dante started singing the first thing that came into his head: the school fight song.

Rally sons of Philomena!
Sing her glory and sound her fame!
Raise her Gold and Blue
And cheer with voices true!
Rah, rah, for Philomena!

We will fight in every game,
Strong of heart and true to her name.
We will ne'er forget her
And will cheer her ever
Loyal to Philomena.

"Dante?" Miranda said, her soft fingers touching his bare knee. He jumped and stopped singing.

"Don't stop!" yelled Vincent, now on the other side of the room—he'd definitely passed Dante somehow. Miranda quickly started humming the fight song again.

They heard a clatter nearby and then the sound of something rolling away.

"Must have been a cleaning cart or—"

A hand grabbed Dante's head and a knee banged into his back.

"Oh, there you are," said Spangler, settling down next to Dante. "Now, let's see what you have."

"Wait for me!" Vincent bellowed, now directly opposite them.

"Vincent, you're going in a circle!" said Miranda.

"I know that—the room is a big circle!" Vincent yelled.

Everyone was puzzled for a moment. "Are you hanging onto the wall?" asked Miranda. Vincent didn't answer. "We're somewhere in the middle of the room," said Miranda. "You're going to have to let go of the wall and come out here where we are."

They heard a few shuffling steps. "C'mon, that's right," Miranda coaxed. She kept talking until Vincent finally tripped over Dante. Miranda grabbed him and pulled him down next to her. He was shaking. She held his hand and murmured soothing things. Dante tried not to pay attention to them.

The whole time, Dante had been running his fingers around the tiles where he could feel the most vibration. Now he thought he could feel one shifting back and forth.

"Here, feel," he said to Spangler and guided his hand to the tile.

"I feel it!" said Spangler. "Keep your hand there while I find—yes, my pocket knife. Let's see now . . . ah! I have an edge lifted. Dante, can you—"

With a scraping sound, Dante tipped the tile up, then pulled it out. Cautiously he put his hand into the hole. He felt smooth metal and then—

"It's a lock—a combination lock just like on the lockers!" He put his hand on the knob, then snatched it back, keeping his fingers resting lightly on the metal plate.

"Vincent, your watch!" said Miranda. Suddenly her face shone green in the light from the watch.

"Of course! A Casio G-Shock lights up," said Vincent, his voice sounding almost normal. "Wish I'd thought of that a while ago."

Suddenly the metal beneath Dante's fingers burned hot.

"We've got to get it open!" Dante screamed.

"How? We haven't the faintest idea of what the combination is," Spangler replied.

The building slowly slipped about three feet lower. The custodian's cart began to roll toward them again as the floor tilted.

"Do something!" Vincent screamed.

Miranda was obsessively crumpling a piece of paper in her pocket as her mind raced. They were so close. *Think, Miranda!*

The paper in her pocket was beginning to come apart from the sweat on her palms.

A small crack in the floor directly in front of the huddled four suddenly became three inches wide, and sulfurous steam rose from it.

And then there were the screams, now just barely audible from below them.

Miranda pulled her hand from her pocket to cover her mouth. The paper fluttered out, settling just within the pathetic glow of Vincent's watch.

"Vincent! Light, I need the light!" She grabbed his arm and twisted it over the paper, which read:

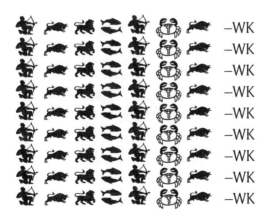

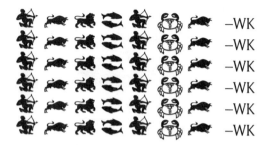

							–WK
							–WK
							–WK
							–WK
							–WK
							–WK

"It's the combo! 'WK' is Wassily Konstantinos. He gave us the combo! Somehow, he gave us the answer!" She was shaking the paper in Dante's face.

Dante didn't need more explanation. He grabbed the paper and Vincent's wrist.

"That hurts! Careful!" Vincent yelped.

They stared at the dial. Steam was now erupting from the floor like a geyser.

"Not to put undue pressure on anyone, but I think we've got precisely one chance to get this right," said Spangler.

The building rocked suddenly sideways, tilting the floor almost forty-five degrees. Spangler and Dante slid away and landed against the wall. Miranda grabbed for the hole and Vincent's wrist. The cleaning cart came careening back toward them, smashing into

Vincent and tearing him out of Miranda's grasp.

"Vincent!" Miranda screamed, still clinging to the hole.

"Oof," said Vincent as he hit the wall, the cart clanging next to him. "Miranda, you have my watch! Use it for light and do the combination! Now!"

"I don't have the paper!" Miranda wailed.

"I do!" said Dante—he hadn't even realized it was still in his hand. "Oh, but I can't see."

"I remember it!" said Vincent. "Archer, bull—"

"I can't," cried Miranda. "I've never been able to open a locker at this school, ever. I just can't do it!"

"C'mon, Jellybean, you can do it," said Vincent.

"Miranda, you're the smartest person I know," said Dante, his voice cracking. "We need you."

Miranda sniffed, then said. "Watch out, here come my shoes. I need better traction to pull myself up closer." They heard her shoes slide down and hit the wall. They could hear her scrambling, then they saw the glow of Vincent's watch. Miranda was propped on her elbows, clutching the watch with one hand. Her other her hand was on the knob. She looked grim.

"OK," she said.

"Start at the empty spot," said Vincent.

"It is," she answered.

"Turn left until you get to the guy with the bow."

"Left, left," Miranda muttered. "OK."

"Now turn right to the bull."

"OK."

"Left to the lion."

"OK."

"Right to the fish."

"Got it."

"Left to the scorpion. . . . right to the crab."

"OK."

"Now, very carefully, go all the way around again, turning right, and then stop at the bull again."

"Wait, do you always have to go all the way around first?" demanded Miranda.

"Uh, yeah," said Vincent and Dante.

"Well, no one ever told me that! Maybe that's been my problem with these stupid lockers! You have no idea how much time I've spent—"

"Uh, Jellybean, could you finish the combination and see if it saves the day?" broke in Vincent.

"Oh, sorry."

They held their breaths as Miranda turned the knob and positioned the last symbol.

Dante's mother was glued to the local morning show again. A way-too-wide-awake reporter was standing in front of a smoking crater.

The reporter spoke, "Police and federal disaster officials remain on scene at the site of St. Philomena High School in Bridgewater, where a seismic disaster of, frankly, biblical proportions took place two days ago.

"What was once Bridgewater's architectural pride and joy is now just a hole in the ground.

The building began to sink and to split in two sometime Monday morning. Some of our local history buffs may remember that the school was built over a sizable sinkhole. However, great care was taken by the famed architect Ivor Shandor to make sure the school was stable and safe. No one is sure what changed or what caused the building to drop halfway into the sinkhole. Investigators are combing the little remaining wreckage for clues.

"What's most remarkable, though, is that all but one of the four hundred students, faculty, and staff are accounted for at this time. Students, faculty, and staff began streaming out shortly after rescue crews arrived on the scene. They were led by three students whom we've managed to identify as Miranda Lee, Dante Grant, and Vincent Young.

"Our reporter on the scene tried to ask what happened inside the school, but only Grant responded, saying 'You wouldn't believe us if we told you.'

"However, we are joined now by Dr. Giles Spangler, who only yesterday was telling us all about the school's architect, Ivor Shandor. Now

Dr. Spangler, yesterday you mentioned Ivor Shandor's interest in the occult—"

Before his mother could ask him any more questions—she'd been trying nonstop to get him to talk since he got home early yesterday—Dante grabbed his bag and slipped out the door. Nothing Spangler had to say would be news to him, anyway.

Obviously, there were no classes at St. Philomena that day. The administrators were hard at work figuring out where classes could be held until a new school was built. A plan would be announced next Monday.

Although he knew there was nothing there, Dante's feet automatically took him on his regular route to school.

Even from a distance he could see the yellow police tape where the school used to be. He stood across the street from the building and stared. It already seemed like just a bad dream.

He was turning to leave when his eye was caught by someone standing under the trees just outside the police line. It was Miranda! He waved and began to jog over. This, he knew now, was why he'd come here.

"Miranda!" he called as he crossed the parking lot. She turned and smiled. Dante felt so happy. He stopped feeling happy as soon as he saw Vincent was sitting on the ground next to Miranda. Dante stopped running. He walked up to them slowly.

"I was hoping we'd see you here," said Miranda. Dante grunted.

"Vincent thinks we could have suffered a mass hallucination." They all gazed at the crater in front of them.

"It's all over the news," Dante finally said.

"Yeah, I saw," said Vincent unexpectedly. "I liked your statement, man. But Spangler's blabbing all about it."

Dante shrugged.

Miranda touched his arm. "You were great, Dante," she said softly. "We never would have gotten everyone out if it weren't for you." She had tears in her eyes.

"You were great, too," said Dante, trying to control his voice. Miranda gave him a watery smile.

"Hey, hey, I provided some illumination, remember?" said Vincent, standing up and moving closer to Miranda.

She looked away and wiped her eyes. "I know it's weird, but I feel bad that Mrs. Konstantinos didn't make it out."

Dante and Vincent nodded, not knowing what to say.

"Well, I should—I think there's practice today later," said Dante finally, jamming his hands in his pockets. "I'll see you later." He started to walk away.

"Hey! Dante! You should think about the Numismatic Club when we sign up for extracurriculars next week. We'd love to have ya!" Vincent yelled.

Dante waved and turned away. He thought he saw a figure in black inside the police tape. He shook his head and just kept walking.

Epilogue

Principal Jones could hardly believe it when he tore open the envelope. It had arrived by special delivery at his temporary office at St. Philomena Middle School. Inside was a check and note. The note was written in flowing handwriting on old, yellowed paper: "For the new St. Philomena, to be built on the ruins of the old." A bank in Moldova had issued the check. For ten million dollars.

Jones's mouth was still wide open in shock when someone knocked at the door. "Come—come in," he stuttered.

A woman in black emerged from the dark hallway. "Principal Jones," she said, "I understand your new school will need a qualified librarian."

Everything's fine in Bridgewater. Really . . .

Or is it?

Look for all the titles from the
Night Fall collection.

THE CLUB

Bored after school, Josh and his friends decide to try out an old board game. The group chuckles at Black Magic's promises of good fortune. But when their luck starts skyrocketing—and horror strikes their enemies—the game stops being funny. How can Josh stop what he's unleashed? Answers lie in an old diary—but ending the game may be deadlier than any curse.

THE COMBINATION

Dante only thinks about football. Miranda's worried about applying to college. Neither one wants to worry about a locker combination too. But they'll have to learn their combos fast—if they want to survive. Dante discovers that an insane architect designed St. Philomena High, and he's made the school into a doomsday machine. If too many kids miss their combinations, no one gets out alive.

FOUL

Rhino is one of Bridgewater best basketball players— except when it comes to making free throws. It's not a big deal, until he begins receiving strange threats. If Rhino can't make his shots at the free throw line, someone will start hurting the people around him. Everyone's a suspect: a college recruiter, Rhino's jealous best friend, and the father Rhino never knew—who recently escaped from prison.

LAST DESSERTS

Ella loves to practice designs for the bakery she'll someday own. She's also one of the few people not to try the cookies and cakes made by a mysterious new baker. Soon the people who ate the baker's treats start acting oddly, and Ella wonders if the cookies are to blame. Can her baking skills help her save her best friend—and herself?

THE LATE BUS

Lamar takes the "late bus" home from school after practice each day. After the bus's beloved driver passes away, Lamar begins to see strange things—demonic figures, preparing to attack the bus. Soon he learns the demons are after Mr. Rumble, the freaky new bus driver. Can Lamar rescue his fellow passengers, or will Rumble's past come back to destroy them all?

LOCK-IN

The Fresh Start Lock-In was supposed to bring the students of Bridgewater closer together. Jackie didn't think it would work, but she didn't think she'd have to fight for her life, either. A group of outsider kids who like to play werewolf might not be playing anymore. Will Jackie and her brother escape Bridgewater High before morning? Or will a pack of crazed students take them down?

MESSAGES FROM BEYOND

Some guy named Ethan has been texting Cassie. He seems to know all about her—but she can't place him. Cassie thinks one of her friends is punking her. But she can't ignore how Ethan looks just like the guy in her nightmares. The search for Ethan draws her into a struggle for her life. Will Cassie be able to break free from her mysterious stalker?

THE PRANK

Pranks make Jordan nervous. But when a group of popular kids invite her along on a series of practical jokes, she doesn't turn them down. As the pranks begin to go horribly wrong, Jordan and her crush Charlie work to discover the cause of the accidents. Is the spirit of a prank victim who died twenty years earlier to blame? And can Jordan stop the final prank, or will the haunting continue?

THE PROTECTORS

Luke's life has never been "normal." His mother holds séances and his crazy stepfather works as Bridgewater's mortician. But living in a funeral home never bothered Luke—until his mom's accident. Then the bodies in the funeral home start delivering messages to him, and Luke is certain he's going nuts. When they start offering clues to his mother's death, he has no choice but to listen.

SKIN

It looks like a pizza exploded on Nick Barry's face. But a bad rash is the least of his problems. Something sinister is living underneath Nick's skin. Where did it come from? What does it want? With the help of a dead kid's diary, Nick slowly learns the answers. But there's still one question he must face: how do you destroy an evil that's inside you?

THAW

A storm caused a major power outage in Bridgewater. Now a project at the Institute for Cryogenic Experimentation is ruined, and the thawed-out bodies of twenty-seven federal inmates are missing. At first, Dani didn't think much of the news. Then her best friend Jake disappeared. To get him back, Dani must enter a dangerous alternate reality where a defrosted inmate is beginning to act like a god.

UNTHINKABLE

Omar Phillips is Bridgewater High's favorite local teen author. His Facebook fans can't wait for his next horror story. But lately Omar's imagination has turned against him. Horrifying visions of death and destruction come at him with wide-screen intensity. The only way to stop the visions is to write them down. Until they start coming true . . .

SOUTHSIDE HIGH

ARE YOU A SURVIVOR?

Check out all the books in the

SURVIVING SOUTH SIDE

collection.

Bad Deal

Fish hates taking his ADHD meds. They help him concentrate, but they also make him feel weird. When a cute girl needs a boost to study for tests, Fish offers her a pill. Soon more kids want pills, and Fish likes the profits. To keep from running out, Fish finds a doctor who sells phony prescriptions. After the doctor is arrested, Fish decides to tell the truth. But will that cost him his friends?

Beaten

Paige is a cheerleader. Ty's a football star. They seem like the perfect couple. But when they have their first fight, Ty scares Paige with his anger. Then after losing a game, Ty goes ballistic and hits Paige. Ty is arrested for assault, but Paige still secretly meets up with him. What's worse—flinching every time your boyfriend gets angry, or being alone?

Benito Runs

Benito's father has been in Iraq for over a year. When he returns, Benito's family life is not the same. Dad suffers from PTSD—post-traumatic stress disorder—and yells constantly. Benito can't handle seeing his dad so crazy, so he decides to run away. Will Benny find a new life? Or will he learn how to deal with his dad—through good times and bad?

PLAN B

Lucy has her life planned: she'll graduate high school and join her boyfriend at college in Austin. She'll become a Spanish teacher and of course they'll get married. So there's no reason to wait to sleep together, right? They try to be careful, but Lucy gets pregnant. Lucy's plan is gone. How will she make the most difficult decision of her life?

RECRUITED

Kadeem is Southside High's star quarterback. College scouts are seeking him out. One recruiter even introduces him to a college cheerleader and gives him money to have a good time. But then officials start to investigate illegal recruiting. Will Kadeem decide to help their investigation, though it means the end of the good times? What will it do to his chances of playing in college?

SHATTERED STAR

Cassie is the best singer at Southside. She dreams of being famous. Cassie skips school to try out for a national talent competition. But her hopes sink when she sees the line. Then a talent agent shows up and tells Cassie she has "the look" he wants. Soon she is lying and missing glee club rehearsal to meet with him. And he's asking her for more each time. How far will Cassie go for her shot at fame?